Yummers Too

The Second Course

James Marshall

Houghton Mifflin Company   Boston

To M.F.K. Fisher

Library of Congress Cataloging-in-Publication Data

Marshall, James, 1942—
  Yummers too.

  Summary: Emily Pig tries to earn money to pay off
debts created by her love of food, but her large appetite
keeps getting in the way.
  [1. Pigs—Fiction] I. Title.
PZ7.M35672Yu 1986   [E]   86-10667
ISBN 0-395-38990-9

Printed in the United States of America

RNF ISBN 0-395-38990-9
PAP ISBN 0-395-53967-6

WOZ 10 9 8

Emily Pig was settling down for a long siesta.

"I'm going to stay here all afternoon," she said.

"Popsicles!" called out Eugene.

"Come and get your ice-cold Popsicles!"

Emily was up in a flash.

She ate three raspberry Popsicles in a row.

"Simply yummers," she said.

"That will be sixty cents, please,"
said Eugene.

"I beg your pardon?" said Emily.

"Sixty cents," said Eugene.

"Now see here," said Emily.

"I thought we were *friends!*"

"This is business," said Eugene.

But Emily had spent all her money
at the candy store.
"I don't have sixty cents," she said.
At that moment Uncle Fatty Pig,
Emily's favorite relative, came by.
"May I please have sixty cents?"
said Emily.
But Uncle Fatty had just been
to the pastry shop.
His pockets were empty.
"Why don't you earn it?" he suggested.

"That's a fine idea," said Eugene.
And he gave Emily his cap
and his cart.
"Come back when you've sold
sixty cents worth," he said.
"This won't take long," said Emily.

Emily's first customer
was her friend Connie.
"What's the best flavor?" said Connie.
"That's a good question,"
said Emily.

And she began to sample.

"This banana fudge is tasty," she said.

"And this mocha chip isn't half bad."

Soon there wasn't a Popsicle left.

But that wasn't the worst of it.

"Don't look now," said Connie.

Eugene's cart crashed right into
Healthy Harriet's Health Food Store.
"Popsicles!" cried Harriet.
"How insulting!"
"You'll have to pay for this damage!"
Emily explained that she didn't have
any money.
"I'll think of something," said Harriet.

Emily was put to work
behind the counter.
"Take care of the store until I return,"
said Harriet.
"Don't worry about a thing," said Emily.
When Harriet was gone,
Emily began to look around.
She had never been in a health food store.
"It's important to expand one's tastes,"
she said, reaching into a barrel
of honey-dipped papaya.
"I'll have just one."

Healthy Harriet couldn't believe her eyes.
Emily had eaten all the honey-dipped papaya,
an entire supply of frozen yogurt,
six cans of ginseng pop,
and quite a few carob bars.
"I lost control," she explained.
"So I see," said Harriet.
And she put Emily to work
doing something else.

At the corner of Peach and Pecan streets
there came a sudden gust of wind,
and Emily was airborne.

When the wind died away,

Emily began to descend.

Down below, two bad dogs were stealing

a beautiful wedding cake

from a French bakery.

"Hee, hee," said one bad dog.

"Nothing can stop us now."

Emily crash-landed
and knocked the two bad dogs
out cold.

The bakers were delighted to have
their beautiful wedding cake back unharmed.
They offered Emily a nice cash reward.
"Hot dog," said Emily. "That's *just* enough
to pay back Healthy Harriet and Eugene."
"Or," said the bakers,
"You may have a box of our
special chocolate éclairs.
Take your pick."

"Eclairs?" said Emily.

Eugene was just waking up
from his siesta when Emily returned.
"You were gone a long time," he said.
"I had a busy afternoon," said Emily.
And she gave Eugene a full account.
"A cash reward or chocolate éclairs,"
said Eugene. "That must have been
a difficult decision."
"Yes," said Emily. "There was only
one thing to do."
"And?" said Eugene.

"Have an éclair," said Emily.